From June 2001 until March 2002 I worked as the writer-and-illustrator-in-residence at Tate Britain in London. This was part of a three-year project called Visual Paths, developed by the Tate in partnership with the Institute of Education. I worked with a thousand children from inner-city schools, teaching literacy using the resources within the gallery. My job was to create a new book based on responses to works of art in the Tate collections, and to conduct workshops with the children and their teachers. I remember it as a time that changed my life forever.

I must thank Colin Grigg, Co-ordinator of Visual Paths, who was as inspirational as the paintings, and the children of these schools, who played the shape game so wonderfully (as all children do):

Churchill Gardens Primary School
Gloucester Primary School
Henry Fawcett Primary School
Latham Primary School
Marianne Richardson Primary School
Michael Faraday Primary School
Saint Gabriel's Primary School
Saint Mark's Primary School
Shapla Primary School
Vicarage Primary School
Langdon School

DISCARDED
From Nashville Public Library

NASHVILLE PUBLIC LIBRARY

W9-BYB-800

For my brother Michael, who spent hours playing the shape game with me —A.B.

The Great Day of His Wrath by John Martin © Tate, London, 2002. *Past and Present No. 1* by Augustus Egg © Tate, London, 2002.
The Cholmondeley Ladies by British School seventeenth century © Tate, London, 2002. *The Death of Major Peirson* by John Singleton Copley © Tate, London, 2002.
The Boyhood of Raleigh by Sir John Everett Millais © Tate, London, 2002. *Horse Devoured by a Lion* by George Stubbs © Tate, London, 2002.
Allegro Strepitoso by Carel Weight © Tate, London, 2002. *Self-Portrait with Badges* by Peter Blake © Peter Blake, 1961.
The Meeting or *Have a Nice Day, Mr Hockney* by Peter Blake © Peter Blake, 1981–83.

Copyright © 2003 by A E T Browne & Partners
All rights reserved
Printed and bound in Singapore
First published in Great Britain by Doubleday, an imprint of
Random House Children's Books, 2003
First American edition, 2003
1 3 5 7 9 10 8 6 4 2
Library of Congress Cataloging-in-Publication Data
Browne, Anthony, 1946–
  The shape game / Anthony Browne.— 1st American ed.
    p. cm.
  Summary: The author/illustrator describes how his mother's wish to spend
her birthday visiting an art museum with her family changed the course
of his life forever.
  ISBN 0-374-36764-7
  1. Browne, Anthony, 1946—Childhood and youth—Juvenile literature.
2. Illustrators—Great Britain—Biography—Juvenile literature.   3. Art
museums—Juvenile literature.   4. Art appreciation—Juvenile literature.
[1. Browne, Anthony, 1946—Childhood and youth.   2. Illustrators.
3. Authors, English.   4. Art museums.   5. Art appreciation.]   I. Title.

NC978.5.B768 B76 2003
708—dc21

2002192894

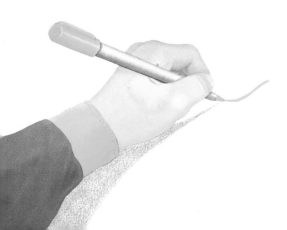

THE SHAPE GAME

Anthony Browne

Farrar Straus Giroux
New York

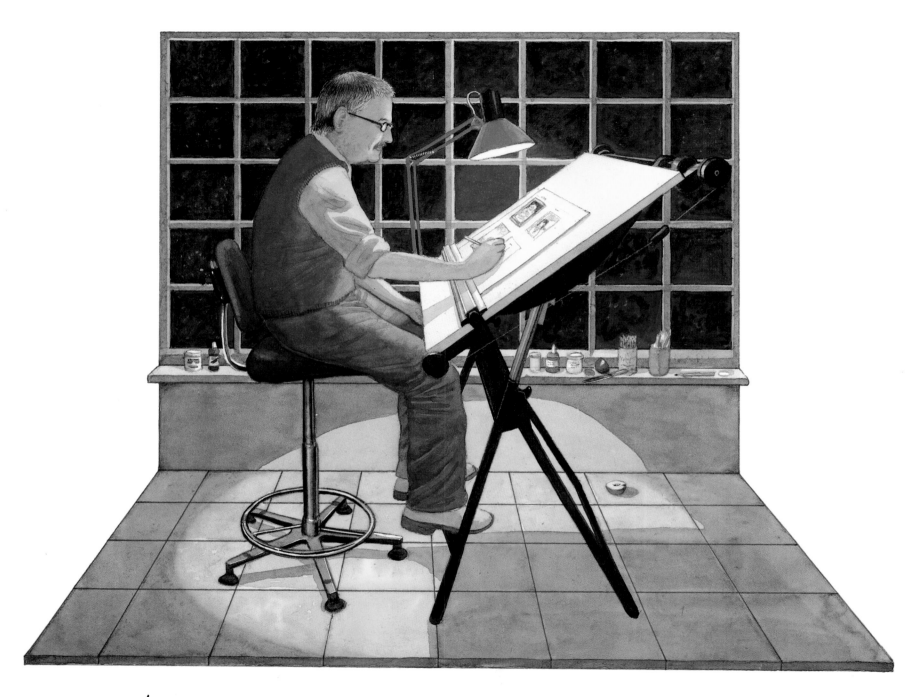

I was a little boy and didn't know what to expect.
It was my mother's idea — that year for her birthday
she wanted us all to go somewhere different.
It turned out to be a day that changed my life forever.

Dad

Mom

George

me

We went on a train to the city and then had a long walk.
There was an important soccer game on the TV, so I knew
Dad and George didn't really want to come. George spent most of
the time trying to trip me up, and Dad told us some of his jokes.

"Why do gorillas have huge nostrils?"

"I don't know," said George.

"Because they've got huge fingers!" said Dad.

All his jokes were like that.

When we got there, the place looked really fancy.

I felt a bit nervous, and even George and Dad were quiet.
(At first.)

"What on earth is that supposed to be?" asked Dad.
"It's supposed to be a mother and child," said Mom.
"Well, why isn't it?" said Dad.

Mom took us into a large room that was full of old paintings.
"Boring," said George, and Dad told him to shut up.
(I thought it looked boring, too, but I wasn't sure.)

George leaned against a picture,
and one of the guards came and told him off.
So Dad told him off, too.
It wasn't a very good start to the visit, especially for George.

John Martin: *The Great Day of His Wrath*

Dad tried to cheer him up: "Did you hear about the
fool who keeps going around saying no?"

"No," George mumbled.

"Oh, so it's you, then!" Dad said, laughing.

George wandered away.

Augustus Egg: *Past and Present No 1*

Mom talked to us about a painting of a family. "Does it remind you of a family we know?" asked Mom, but she was smiling.
She said that the father was holding a love letter written to his wife by another man, and that there were lots of clues in the picture that told us more of the story. So we all worked it out:

Adam and Eve were thrown out of Paradise after Eve was tempted to eat the serpent's apple. The mother was also tempted – by the other man.

In the mirror we can see an open door showing that the mother will have to leave home.

The broken ship is abandoned by its crew, and the man also feels abandoned by his wife.

Portrait of the mother

Portrait of the father

The children's house of cards is falling down, like their happy family life.

Portrait of the other man

The bad half of the apple, like the woman, has fallen to the floor.

The woman has fallen to the floor because she's so upset, and the bracelets on her wrists are painted to look like handcuffs.

"It's gone, gone forever, I tell you!" said Dad.

"What has?" I asked.

"Yesterday!" said Dad.

"Those two are just the same," I said.

"Well, not exactly," said Mom. "Look more closely."

SPOT THE DIFFERENCE

These pictures are not the same — how many differences can you see?

John Singleton Copley: The Death of Major Peirson

From the next room George called, "Hey, look at this — it's GREAT!"
"Do you think so?" said Mom.
"Can you imagine that really happening in our street?"

Sir John Everett Millais: *The Boyhood of Raleigh*

"*D*oes that remind you of anything?" asked Mom.

"It reminds me of Dad telling us one of his jokes," I said.

George Stubbs: *Horse Devoured by a Lion*

"Now, that's what I call a painting," said Dad.
"Look at that lion — it's SO REAL!"

And it was.

Carel Weight: *Allegro Strepitoso*

Peter Blake: *Self-Portrait with Badges*

Peter Blake: *The Meeting or Have a Nice Day, Mr. Hockney*

"Did you hear about the little boy they named after his father?" asked Dad.

"No," I said.

"They called him Dad!" said Dad.

There was a loud silence, but we all started laughing when we saw a painting of a man who looked a bit like Dad.

It was time to go, and on the way out we went to the gift shop. Everything was very expensive, so all we bought were these.

We walked back to get the train, and everyone was in a good mood.
When we got to the station, Dad asked,
"What did Batman say to Robin before they got in the car?"

"Oh, all right then," said Mom. "What did Batman say to
Robin before they got in the car?"

"Robin, get in the car!" replied Dad.

"Come on, boys," said Mom. "Get in the train."

On the way home, Mom showed us a brilliant drawing game that she used to play with her dad. The first person draws a shape — any shape, it's not supposed to be anything, just a shape.

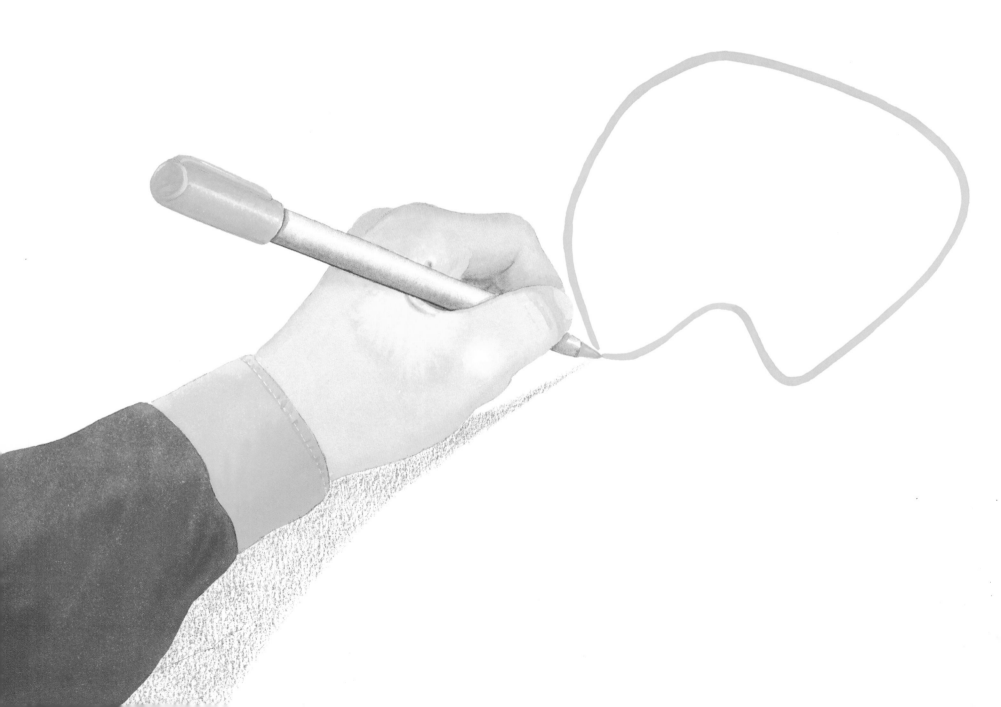

The next person has to change it into something.
It's fantastic. We all played it for the rest of the journey.

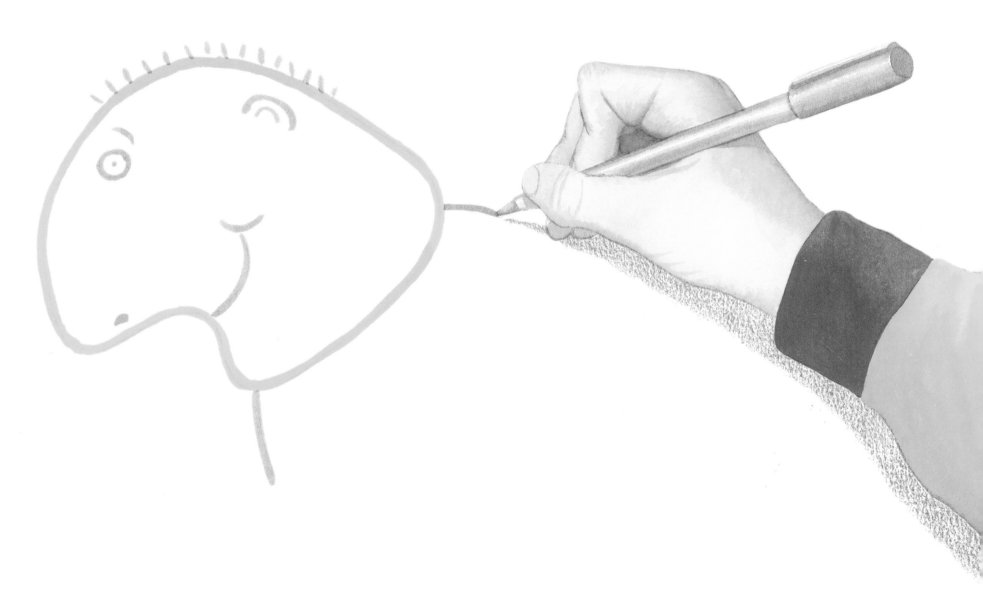

And, in a way, I've been playing the shape game ever since . . .